The Ladybug RACE

By Amy Nielander

Pomegranate Kids®
AGES 3 to 103!

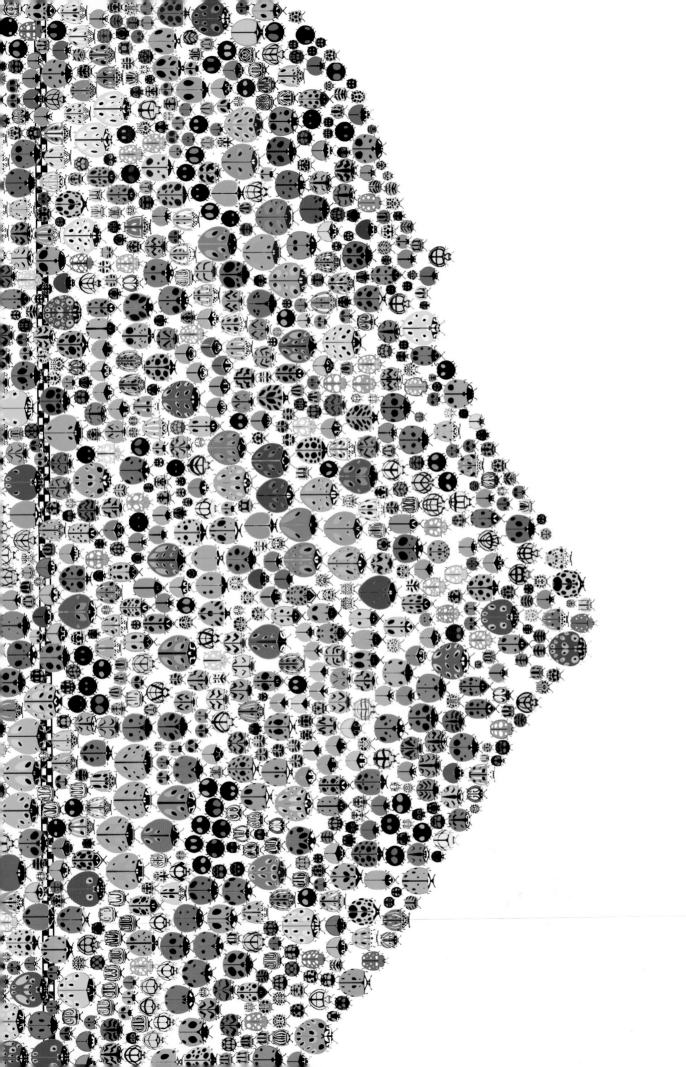

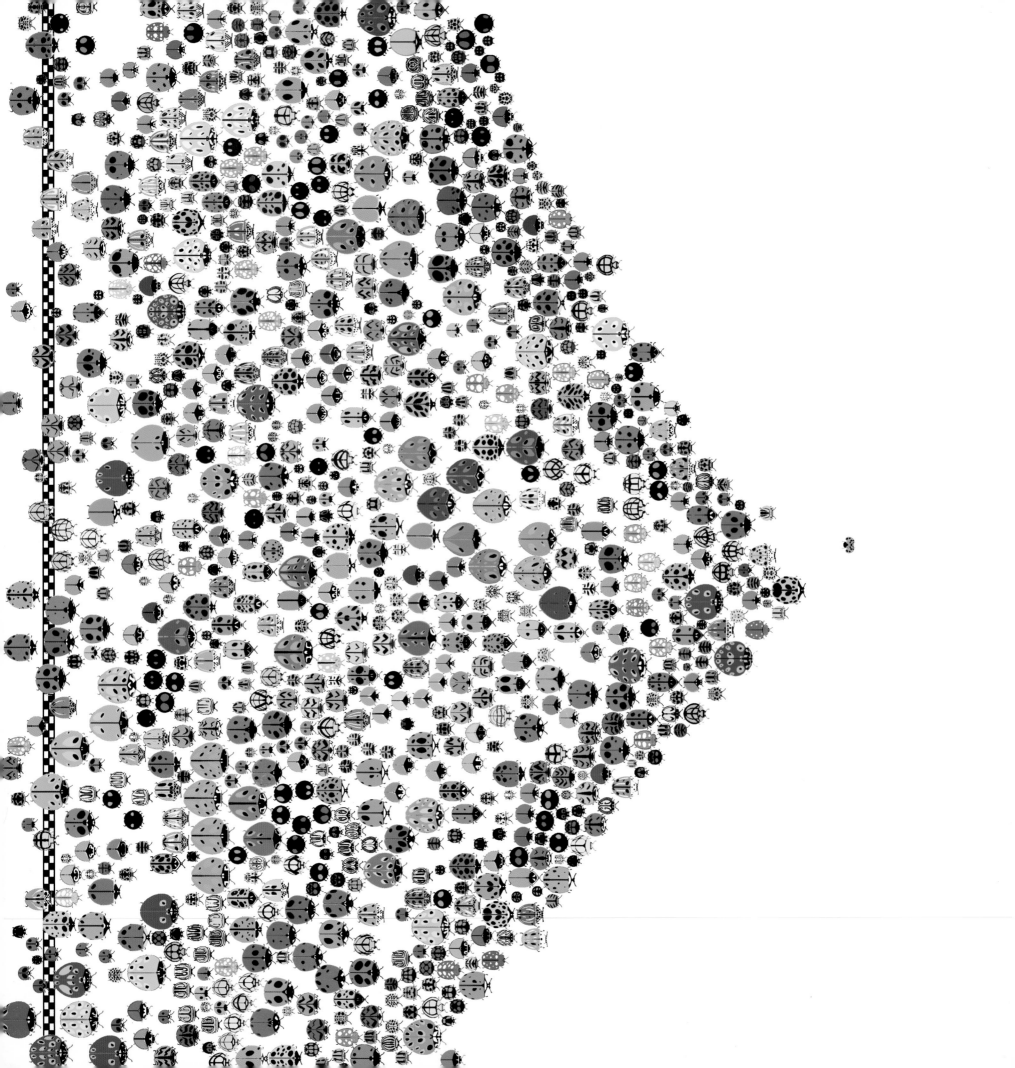

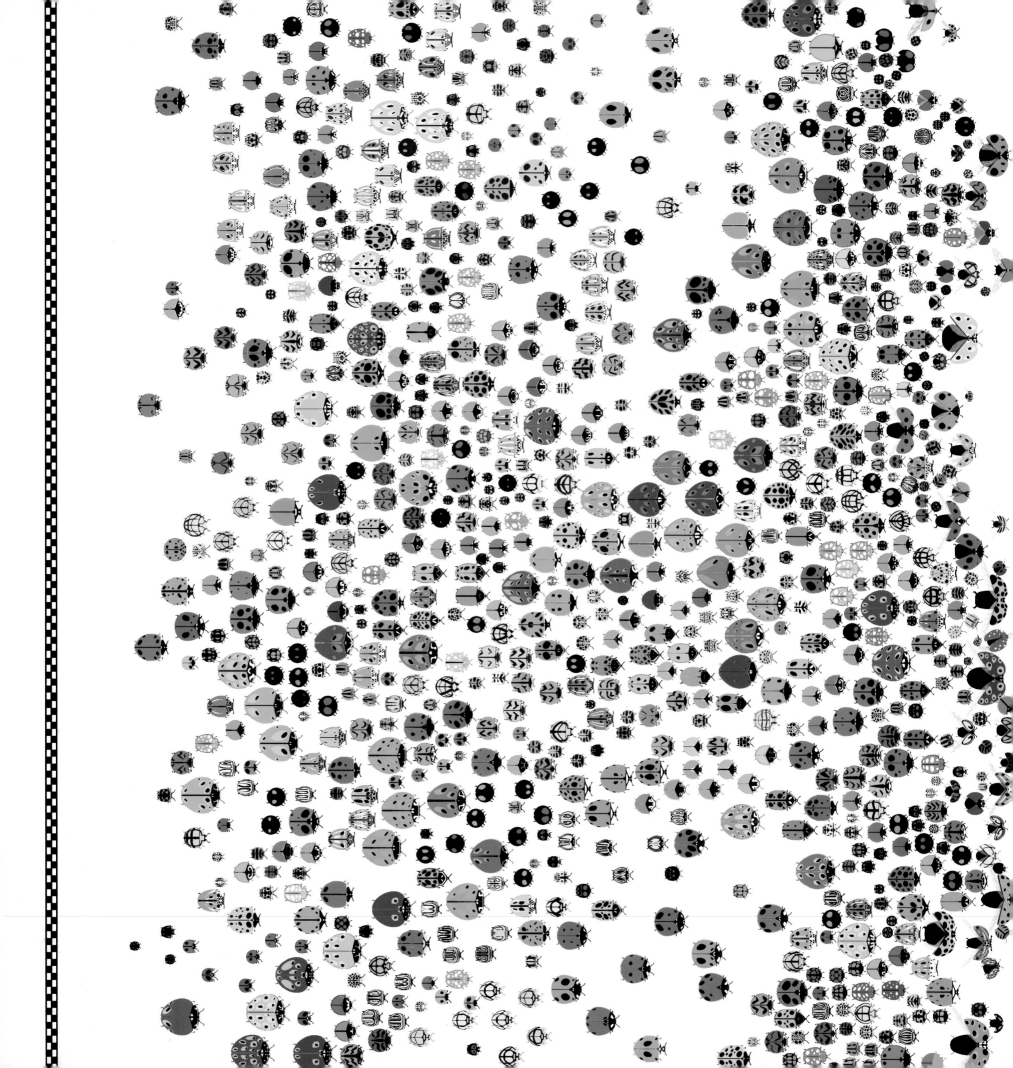

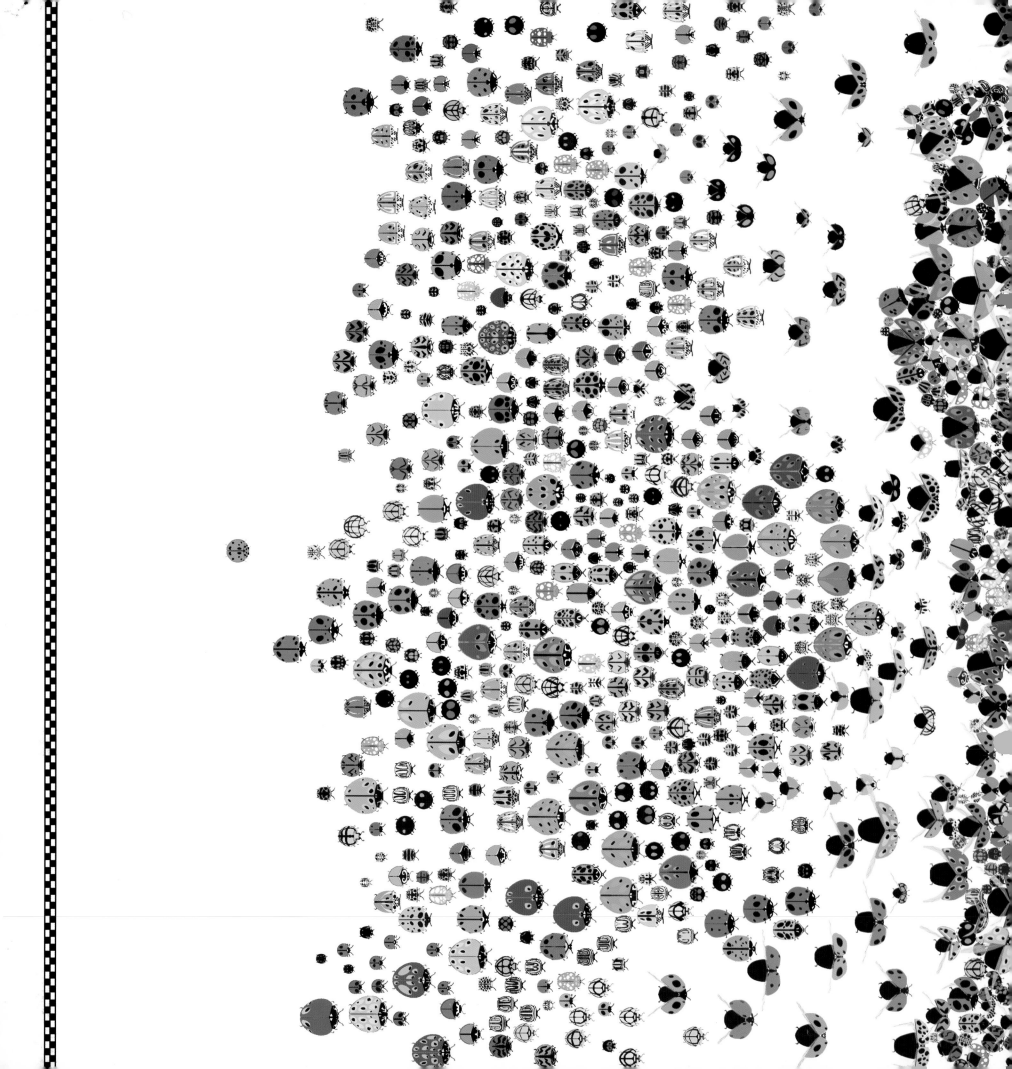

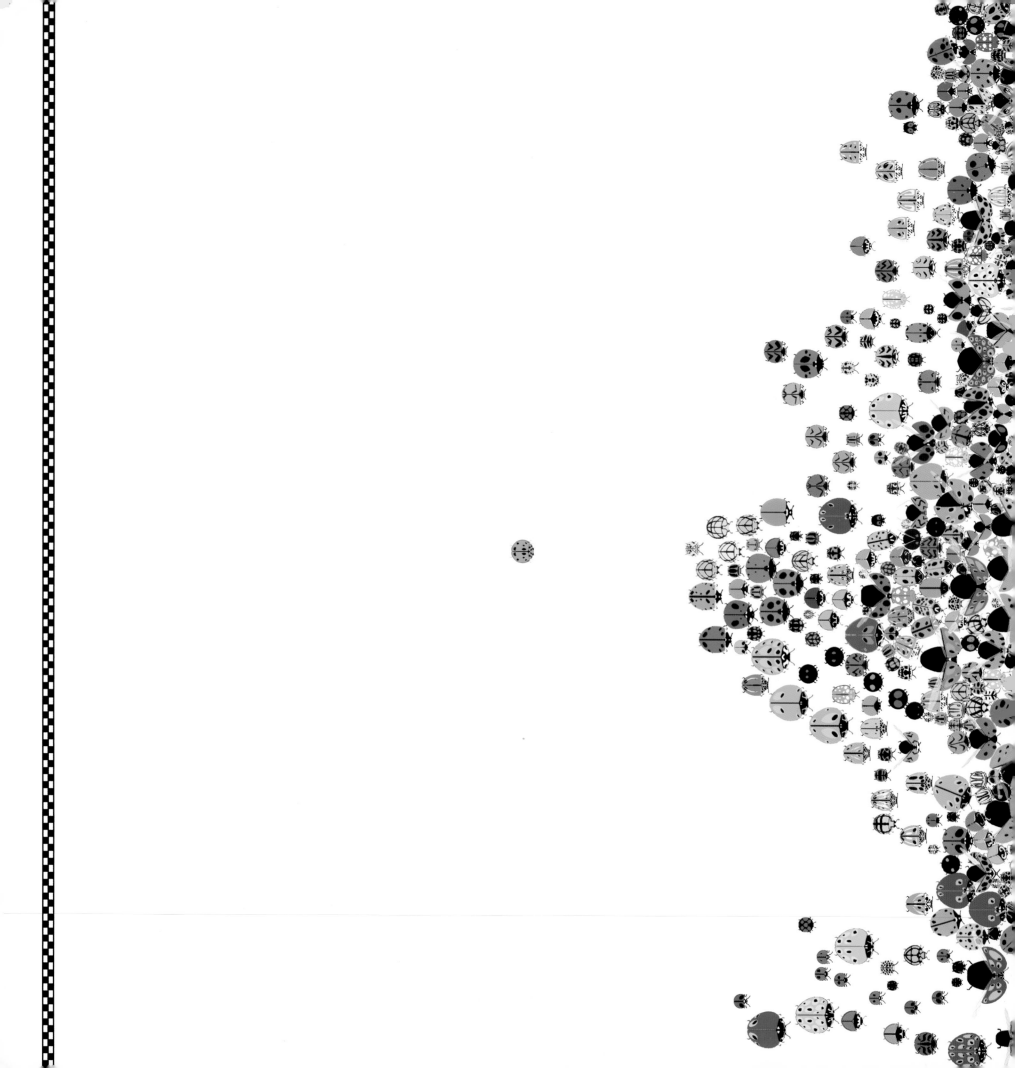

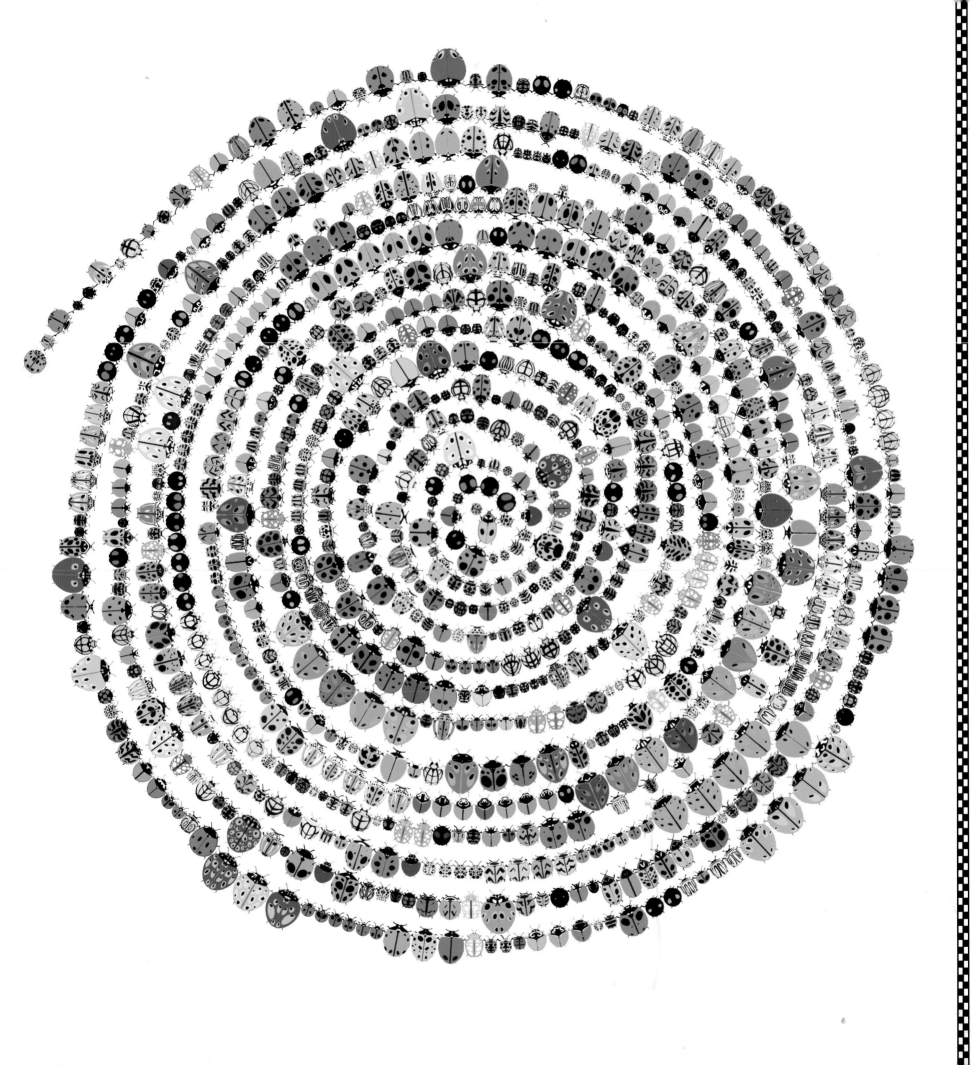

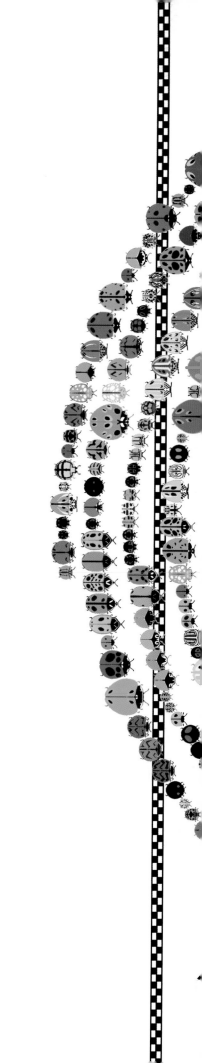

This book is dedicated to Brian, Elliot, and Anna

Amy Nielander is a graduate of the College for Creative Studies in Detroit, Michigan, where she earned a degree in product design. *The Ladybug Race* is her first picture book, and it received international recognition as a Silent Book Contest finalist. All of the ladybugs are rendered true to size.

Amy lives with her husband and two children in Royal Oak, Michigan. They enjoy running a race as a family each year.

You can see more of Amy's work on her website: amynielander.com.

Published by PomegranateKids®, an imprint of Pomegranate Communications, Inc.
19018 NE Portal Way, Portland OR 97230 • 800 227 1428 | www.pomegranate.com

Pomegranate Europe Ltd.
Unit 1, Heathcote Business Centre, Hurlbutt Road, Warwick, Warwickshire CV34 6TD, UK
[+44] 0 1926 430111 • sales@pomeurope.co.uk

To learn about new releases and special offers from Pomegranate,
please visit www.pomegranate.com and sign up for our e-mail newsletter.
For all other queries, see "Contact Us" on our home page.

This product is in compliance with the Consumer Product Safety Improvement Act of 2008 (CPSIA) and any subsequent amendments thereto. A General Conformity Certificate concerning Pomegranate's compliance with the CPSIA is available on our website at www.pomegranate.com, or by request at 800 227 1428. For additional CPSIA-required tracking details, contact Pomegranate at 800 227 1428.

Library of Congress Control Number: 2014958786

ISBN 978-0-7649-7187-7

Item No. A246

Designed by Carey Hall

Printed in China

24 23 22 21 20 19 18 17 16 15   10 9 8 7 6 5 4 3 2 1